The Runaway Bed

The Runaway

To Jared & Chelsey:
Sweet dreams,
Martha Kewenmun

Bed

Martha Newcomer

NEW MILLENNIUM
PRESS

illustrated by Angela Donato

Book design by Carol Tornatore Creative Design

The text of this book is set in Centaur.

The illustrations are rendered in watercolor and ink.

Library of Congress Cataloging-in-Publication Data available from the publisher.

ISBN: 1-893224-46-5

New Millennium Press
301 North Canon Drive
Suite 214
Beverly Hills, CA 90210

First Edition
10 9 8 7 6 5 4 3 2 1

Printed in the United States

Dedicated to my children

who learned to go to bed with this story,

and to the grandchildren who heard it too.

Do you wonder why a BED would run away?

I'm Maggie's bed.

Let me tell you why I ran away.

Maggie is almost four.

We have our own room.

I'm up against the window wall and I'm covered
      with a beautiful patchwork quilt.

I've been in the family for a long time.

Before Maggie was born I spent many years with
      her sisters, Jody and Betsy.

But they are much older now and they have
      their own room down the hall.

Maggie and I have been happy with each other.

We've snuggled together with the plump pillows
      and stuffed animals.

We've always been cozy and warm—
                  until the other night, that is!

There was a sudden rainstorm.
    Thunder boomed.
    Flashes of lightning lit up the sky.

The window was open just enough to blow the curtains,
    chill the room and get me wet.

Maggie woke up.

    She was cold and scared.

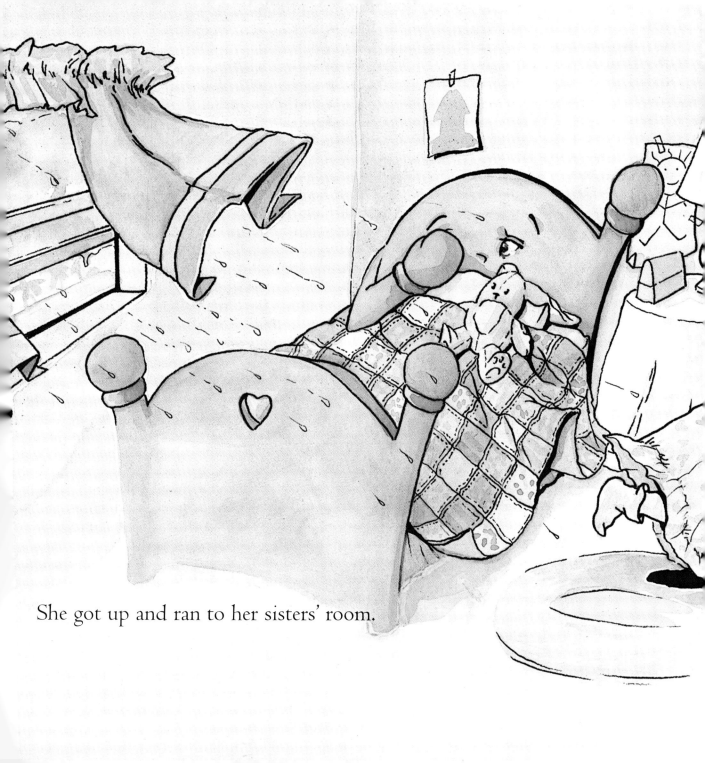

She got up and ran to her sisters' room.

I was left all alone.

I shivered.

I shook.

I felt stiff and lonely,
even unloved.

I had never been left like this before.

Right then and there, I decided to run away.

"Ouch!"
In my rush, I had chipped my leg
as I slid down the stairs and out
the front door.

The dark clouds moved quickly overhead.
The rain stopped as I ran down 39th Avenue.
I turned left on 9th Street North, past Geary's Grocery Store,
Allendale's Drug Store, and Jackie's Photo Mart.

Suddenly...
I thought I saw myself through the window of
Grandma's Attic, the local antique shop!

I was shocked.

It was me all right, but without the patchwork quilt.
I appeared to be wearing a white cotton bedspread.

I took a closer look.

We were the same width, height, and length.
Our legs were identical spindles,
    (except for my new chip).

Our headboards had the same pattern,
    but my twin seemed older, more worn.

MY TWIN . . . was it possible?

As I stood, dazed . . . I saw the fire truck
as it turned from St. Mark's Place.

Fire Chief James rubbed his eyes when he saw me.

He recognized me right away,
    because his wife had made my patchwork quilt
    for Maggie's last birthday, just before Christmas.

The Chief dialed his cell phone.

Then he and Captain Michael lifted me carefully onto their truck.

They took me home.

The whole family was awake by now.
Everyone stood outside to welcome me home.

Maggie was so surprised when she saw me!

When the Chief explained where he had found me,
Maggie's mother remembered:

> "Oh, of course, this bed has a twin! Aunt Kate
> borrowed that bed 30 years ago and we forgot
> all about it," she explained to her husband.

Maggie's mother and father smiled at the memory.
Then, they promised that they would reunite me
> with my twin.

The next day Maggie's mother brought my twin home.
We were pushed together to make one big bed.

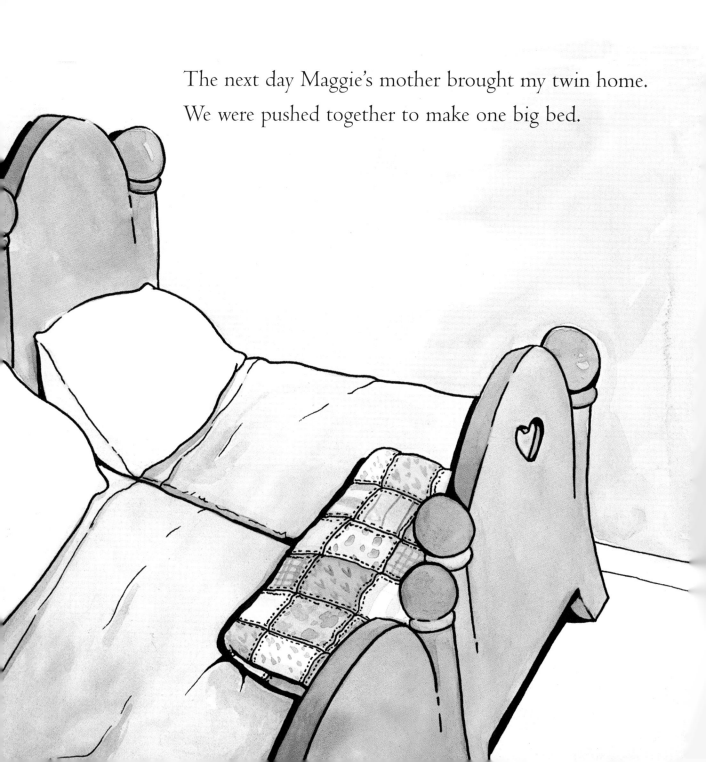

The fire chief's wife promised
to make Maggie a *new* quilt,
one big enough to cover
both of us.

Maggie's promised never to be scared again by thunder and lightning,
and I've promised to never run away again.

Maggie is twice as warm and comfortable now and so am I.

Now we have sweet dreams every night.

For the real Maggie